TO ALL
THE FUTURE
STARGAZERS
EVERYWHERE

CASSANDRA
AND THE
NIGHT SKY

 **bright sky publishing**
HOUSTON, TEXAS

2365 Rice Blvd., Suite 202
Houston, Texas 77005

ISBN: 978-1-942945-74-1

10   9   8   7   6   5   4   3   2   1

Library of Congress Cataloging-in-Publication Data on file with publisher.

Editorial Direction: Lauren Gow
Designer: Marla Y. Garcia

Printed in Canada through Friesens

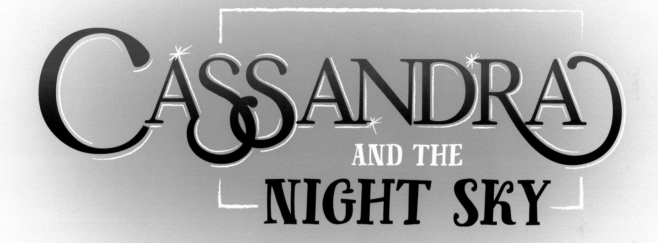

CASSANDRA
AND THE
NIGHT SKY

AMY JACKSON
Illustrations by **DONNA PAREDES**

bright sky publishing
HOUSTON, TEXAS

Once upon a time, there was an evil and greedy king. He sent his royal armies traveling far across the world to bring back all the treasures they could find. He grew greedier and greedier until one day he decided that he would have the most precious treasure of all—the twinkling night sky!

One by one, the twinkling lights went out until one night, they ceased to exist.

Much time passed, and the starry sky faded into bedtime folktales only children believed.

In this kingdom lived a princess named Cassandra, who grew up listening to fables about a time when the stars shined brilliantly.

Her nanny, Rula, spoke of giant figures and shapes in the sky that changed with the turn of the seasons. She spoke of how sailors sailed in sparkling seas, the twinkling lights guiding their ships and illuminating the deep, dark ocean.

The lack of twinkling lights did not concern the princess much.

She was very busy living a royal life. Her days were filled with royal duties and each and every toy she could imagine.

This was a particularly special year, however, for Cassandra was to turn nine.

The special day arrived with a royal celebration, fanfare, and festivities. Cassandra was showered with gifts, yet one gift in particular stood out from the rest. Her nanny gave her a battered old teapot!

"How childish and useless," she thought. "What good can come of that?" Her days of pretend tea parties were over!

"Looks can be deceiving," said her
nanny, Rula, noticing Cassandra's
disapproval. "It is yours and only you
can determine where it will best
be served."

The princess was perplexed.
She didn't understand what
Rula meant, as she was
oblivious to the beauty
that lay sleeping inside.
She gave it to one of the
servant's children after the
party and hoped she would
never see it again.

ne warm summer day, Cassandra found her servant's little daughter pretending to have a tea party with the battered old teapot. "What are you doing here?!" Cassandra yelled at the little girl, "Why are you in my room and why do you have that wretched teapot?"

The little girl stammered, "I just wanted to have a tea party with you and thank you for giving this gift to me!"

Just then, Cassandra started to notice steam coming from the spout of the teapot. They both thought that the teapot was empty. At the same time, both reached to take the lid off to see what was inside.

Their eyes widened as they saw patterns and swirling rainbows of color swimming and shining in a sea of darkness. Cassandra quickly closed the lid, mesmerized by what she saw. Luckily she did, because something else was hidden inside the teapot that was not so pleasant!

"Do you remember the old fables about the evil king who stole the night sky?" Cassandra whispered. "Yes!" answered the little girl. "It is here! He hid it inside the belly of this teapot!" exclaimed Cassandra. "What do we do?" asked the little girl.

"We must bring back the night sky and make it as it once was all those years ago," said Cassandra.

Cassandra picked up the teapot and walked over to the window.

She called down to her longtime guard and companion.

"Cygnus, we need you!"

The graceful swan heard her call, flew from his post in the moat, and perched himself on her windowsill.

Cassandra gallantly climbed onto the swan's back carrying the teapot.

"Fly high into the night sky! Don't stop flying, Cygnus!"

What Cassandra did not know was that the evil, greedy king from long ago had hidden a poisonous scorpion to guard the contents of the teapot in case anyone ever found it.

Her servant's little girl watched Cygnus and Cassandra fly from the windowsill and off into the ink black night sky. Just when she could not see them anymore, Cassandra took the lid off the teapot. A long twinkling stream of steam spread itself across the sky. The stream of steam glowed brightly, lit up by millions of stars.

All at once, the night sky was returned, but to Cassandra's dismay, the last thing to leave the teapot was the scorpion! The scorpion saw its potential prey and started to swing its tail at Cassandra and Cygnus.

Cygnus bravely swooped down and fought off the scorpion as Cassandra held on tight. Cygnus flung the scorpion off into the starry stream of sparkling steam.

"You did it Cygnus," sighed the much relieved Cassandra as she hugged the swan's long neck. With overwhelming joy, Cassandra and Cygnus rose higher and higher up into the sky together.

Wonder and joy enveloped the kingdom
from that day forward. Every summer,
Cassandra, Cygnus, the Teapot, and
the Scorpion share space in the sky for all to see and
remember the bravery of the princess and the swan.

As we look up at the stars at night, we see a multitude of shining stars. Different cultures throughout the ages have wondered about the night sky and made their own star stories to explain the heavens above.

The teapot constellation in the story is also know as Sagittarius the Archer, according to Greek mythology. It is more commonly known as the Teapot. To find it, look south in the sky as night falls in mid to late summer in the Northern Hemisphere.

The steam coming out from the Teapot and reaching across the sky is our very own galaxy, the Milky Way. We are looking into the center of our galaxy during the summertime.

To the right of the Teapot is Scorpius the Scorpion.

Also in Greek mythology, Cassandra is known as Cassiopeia the Queen. She is commonly shown sitting on a throne.

Close by is Cygnus the Swan, flying through the sky with wings outstretched. Cygnus flies close to Cassandra as they circle the Little Dipper throughout the year in the Northern Hemisphere.

Now it's your turn to go outside at night, look up, and connect the stars to make up your very own star stories to share.

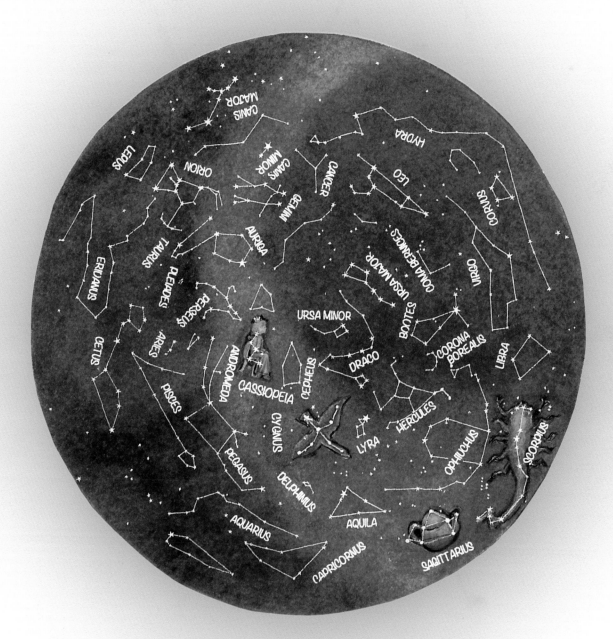

For more information about the night sky, go to www.starryskyaustin.com.
You can even print off your very own constellation map!

ACKNOWLEDGEMENTS

Thank you to all the many Kickstarter campaign contributors who helped us make publishing this story a reality! Special mention to: Roy F. Johnson, Shawn Galloway, and Alida Roca. Thank you to Dr. Juan Carlos Reina, my personal astronomy mentor and friend who not only sparked my interest in astronomy, but also introduced me to my husband. Thank you to all the Starry Sky Austin students who have signed up for my classes over the years. You are the ones who inspired me to write *Cassandra and the Night Sky*. Thank you to my three daughters, Kalen, Piper, and June, for listening to the story develop and helping me polish the book with your ideas. Thank you to my husband for always listening to my many harebrained ideas, and most of all for believing in them and in me. Thank you to my sister, Lori, for her amazing skills of handling logistics and organization for the Kickstarter campaign. She was behind the scenes doing the work that she could do better than us. Thanks to my brother, Eric, for geeking out with me when no one else would. Thank you to my father, Dr. Abel Paredes, who spearheaded the communication and outreach of the Kickstarter campaign. He let me go to Space Camp in the 8th grade and has always supported me in reaching for the stars. And most of all, thank you to my mother, Donna Paredes. I love you Mom! You are such a talented artist! I'm so proud of you!